AN INDIAN HAUNTING

ECHOES OF THE FORGOTTEN

RAVINDERR SINGH

Made with ♥ on the Notion Press Platform
www.notionpress.com

Contents

Foreword

"Shadows linger where light dares not tread."

In this gripping collection of horror stories, **An Indian Haunting,** each tale unravels mysteries that blur the line between the living and the dead. From cursed bridges to haunted lighthouses, restless forests to whispers of bygone souls, these stories weave fear and fascination into every shadow.

Journey through eerie landscapes where ancient secrets rise to claim their due, and humanity's deepest fears are laid bare. With each chilling chapter, you'll question what is real, what is imagined, and what should have been left undisturbed.

Prepare to lose yourself in tales that haunt, thrill, and linger long after the last page.

Preface

"*A storyteller's soul always seeks the extraordinary in the ordinary.*"

Dear Readers,

Thank you for opening this book and stepping into the world of shadows and whispers that I have crafted with care. Growing up in India, I was surrounded by stories—some thrilling, some terrifying, and others simply enchanting. These tales, passed down through generations, ignited a fascination in me for the unknown.

Writing An Indian Haunting,was my way of giving life to these mysteries, blending folklore, personal imagination, and the universal thrill of the supernatural.

This book is for every reader who has ever felt a chill down their spine or wondered about the secrets lurking in the dark. It's my tribute to the magic and mystery that surround us, even when we aren't looking.

This book is my love letter to horror, not just as a genre but as an experience. Fear, after all, connects us—it challenges us, reveals our vulnerabilities, and reminds us of our courage.

I hope you find these tales as thrilling and haunting as I found writing them. May they spark your imagination and perhaps leave you glancing over your shoulder now and then.

Warm regards,
Ravinderr Singh

Prologue

In every corner of the world, there are places where the air feels heavier, the shadows linger longer, and the silence carries an unspoken story. These are the places that intrigue and terrify us, where the line between the living and the departed blurs, and reality bends under the weight of the unknown.

The stories in this book were born from such places—where myth meets truth, and the echoes of the past refuse to fade. They take you to haunted bridges, cursed forests, and forgotten shrines, places where time and space seem to warp, and where those who dare to tread find themselves entangled in mysteries far greater than they imagined.

This book is an invitation to explore these liminal spaces, to embrace the fear that comes from stepping into the unknown, and to find beauty in the dark corners of imagination. Each tale is a doorway to a world where shadows have secrets and whispers hold truths.

So, reader, step cautiously into the pages ahead. Let the stories draw you in, but beware—for the shadows you find here may follow you long after the book is closed.

And remember: every whisper has a story.

Shadows of the Banyan Tree

Chapter 1: The Mysterious Call

It was a humid evening in the small town of Ranikhet, nestled in the Himalayan foothills. The air was thick with the scent of pine and damp earth, and the sound of cicadas filled the twilight. Meera, a 19-year-old college student, had just returned home after spending the day with her friends. Her family lived in an old colonial-style house on the outskirts of the town, surrounded by dense forests and an ancient banyan tree that stood tall in their backyard.

The banyan tree had been there for as long as Meera could remember. Its sprawling roots snaked across the ground, and its twisted branches formed eerie shapes in the moonlight. Locals often whispered about the tree, claiming it was haunted, but Meera never paid much attention to their stories.

As she entered the house, her mother, Aarti, greeted her with a warm smile. "You're late again. Dinner's getting cold," she said, setting the table.

"Sorry, Ma," Meera replied, placing her bag on the sofa. "We were working on our project. I lost track of time."

The family of three sat down to eat. Meera's father, Rajesh, was a schoolteacher with a deep love for history. He often shared stories about the town's past, including tales of British officers and hidden treasures. That evening, however, the conversation was interrupted by an unexpected phone call.

The landline rang sharply, breaking the quiet of the house. Rajesh answered it, his expression turning serious as he listened. "Who's this? Hello?" he said, but there was no response, just the faint sound of static. He hung up, shaking his head. "Must be a prank."

But Meera felt uneasy. Something about the call didn't sit right with her. As the family finished dinner, the wind outside picked up, making the branches of the banyan tree sway. It almost seemed alive, its shadow stretching across the living room window.

That night, as Meera lay in bed, she couldn't shake the feeling that someone was watching her. Her room faced the backyard, and the banyan tree's silhouette loomed against the moonlit sky. She tried to focus on her book, but her thoughts kept drifting back to the phone call and the strange atmosphere.

Just as she was about to turn off the light, she heard a soft tapping sound. It was faint, almost as if someone was gently knocking on her window. Her heart raced as she froze in place, listening intently. The tapping grew louder, more insistent.

Gathering her courage, Meera got out of bed and approached the window. Her hands trembled as she pulled back the curtain. To her relief, there was no one there. But as she looked closer, she noticed something unusual. On the glass were handprints, faint and smudged, as if someone had pressed their palms against it from the outside.

Meera's breath caught in her throat. She opened the window and leaned out, scanning the backyard. The banyan tree's branches swayed in the wind, casting ominous shadows. The air felt colder than usual, and a strange hush had fallen over the forest. She quickly shut the window and locked it, her mind racing.

The rest of the night passed in restless sleep, filled with unsettling dreams of the banyan tree and shadowy figures. When morning came, Meera decided she couldn't ignore the unease any longer. She needed to find out what was going on—and why the banyan tree seemed to hold the answers.

Chapter 2: Whispers in the Wind

The next day, Meera woke up determined to uncover the mystery surrounding the banyan tree. Her first step was to speak to her grandmother, who lived in the old family home in the heart of the town. Dadi, as everyone called her, was known for her wisdom and knowledge of local legends.

After breakfast, Meera told her parents she was heading into town and walked the cobbled streets to her grandmother's house. The morning sun cast long shadows, and the air buzzed with the chatter of shopkeepers and the hum of passing scooters. But even amidst the town's lively rhythm, Meera felt a sense of unease, as though unseen eyes were watching her.

When she reached Dadi's house, the elderly woman welcomed her with open arms. "Meera beta, what brings you here so early?"

"Dadi, I need to ask you something," Meera said, sitting beside her on the verandah. "It's about the banyan tree in our backyard."

Dadi's expression grew serious. She set her teacup down and leaned closer. "That tree... it's not an ordinary one. It's been there for over two centuries, maybe more. The villagers believe it's cursed."

Meera's curiosity deepened. "Cursed? Why?"

Dadi sighed. "They say a spirit lives in that tree, bound there by a powerful ritual. Long ago, a tantrik tried to harness its power, but something went wrong. The spirit became trapped, and since then, strange things have happened around that tree. People hear whispers, see shadows... some even claim to have been touched by invisible hands."

A chill ran down Meera's spine as she listened. She thought of the handprints on her window and the eerie tapping. "Has anyone tried to... get rid of it?"

"Many have tried, but the tree always survives," Dadi said. "It's best to leave it alone."

But Meera wasn't convinced. She thanked her grandmother and left, her mind racing with questions. If the tree was cursed, what did it want? And why was it reaching out to her now?

Chapter 3: A Stranger Appears

Back at home, Meera's thoughts were interrupted by the arrival of a stranger. A man in his early thirties, dressed in simple clothes and carrying a leather satchel, knocked on their door. He introduced himself as Kabir, a historian researching local legends.

"I heard about the banyan tree in your backyard," Kabir said. "It's said to be one of the oldest in the region. Do you mind if I take a look?"

Meera's parents welcomed him in, intrigued by his interest. While Kabir spoke to Rajesh about the tree's historical significance, Meera couldn't shake the feeling that he knew more than he was letting on. His questions were too specific, his gaze too intent.

Later that evening, as Kabir examined the tree, he turned to Meera. "You've felt it, haven't you? The presence?"

Meera's breath hitched. "How do you know?"

Kabir's expression was grim. "Because I've seen it before. This tree isn't just cursed—it's a gateway. And something is trying to come through."

Chapter 4: The Forgotten Diary

The next day, Kabir returned with an old leather-bound diary. "This belonged to a British officer stationed here during the colonial era," he explained. "He was obsessed with the banyan tree and recorded strange events."

The diary detailed eerie occurrences: animals disappearing, shadowy figures, and whispers in the wind. It also mentioned the tantrik who had tried to use the tree's power. "The officer wrote about a ritual to contain the spirit," Kabir said. "But it requires someone to confront the entity."

Kabir and Meera spent hours poring over the diary's entries. They discovered descriptions of how the officer tried to document the tantrik's ritual, and how he failed to stop the spirit from becoming more restless. The officer's last entries hinted at his descent into madness, claiming the tree was "speaking to him" and "showing him things he could not unsee."

Meera felt a growing dread. "Why me?"

"The spirit has chosen you," Kabir said. "You've already felt its presence. It won't stop until you face it."

Chapter 5: The First Encounter

That night, Meera dreamed of the banyan tree. In her dream, a shadowy figure called her name, beckoning her to come closer. She woke up to find the window wide open, though she had locked it before bed. The whispers were louder now, filling her room.

Gathering her courage, Meera went outside. The tree's roots seemed to pulse with a dark energy. As she approached, a sudden gust of wind knocked her back. She caught a glimpse of a face in the bark—anguished and desperate. The air grew colder, and a whisper reached her ears. "Help me," it said.

Terrified, Meera ran back inside and locked the doors. She told Kabir everything, and he confirmed that the spirit was reaching out, trying to make contact. "It's testing you," he said. "You need to be prepared."

Chapter 6: The Ritual

Kabir and Meera prepared for the ritual. They gathered items mentioned in the diary: holy water, sacred herbs, and a talisman. Dadi, despite her initial hesitation, provided guidance, warning Meera of the risks. "The spirit will try to deceive you," she said. "You must hold on to what is real."

The ritual required Meera to face the spirit at midnight when its power would be strongest. Kabir marked a sacred circle around the banyan tree using the herbs, creating a boundary that the spirit couldn't cross. "This circle will protect us," he said. "But you must stay inside it no matter what."

As the hour approached, the air grew heavy, and an unnatural stillness fell over the surroundings. Even the crickets had gone silent. Meera felt her heart pound as she stepped into the circle. The tree's gnarled roots seemed to writhe in the dim light of the lanterns they had placed around the perimeter.

Kabir began chanting verses from the diary, his voice steady and commanding. The words seemed to resonate in the air, carrying a power that made the shadows around the tree dance. Meera held the talisman tightly, her eyes fixed on the bark of the banyan tree, where faint outlines of faces seemed to emerge and fade.

Suddenly, a cold wind swept through the clearing, and a low, guttural whisper echoed around them. "Why have you come?" the voice asked, deep and menacing. A shadowy figure began to take form, rising from the base of the tree. Its eyes glowed like embers, and its presence exuded an overwhelming sense of dread.

"You will not harm anyone anymore," Kabir said firmly, continuing his chant. He motioned for Meera to step forward. "Now, Meera. Speak to it."

Meera's voice trembled as she addressed the spirit. "Why are you here? What do you want?"

The spirit's eyes locked onto hers, and for a moment, everything else seemed to fade away. "I was betrayed," it said, its voice filled with sorrow and rage. "My soul was bound to this tree by those who feared my power. They sought to control me, but they left me to suffer for eternity."

Meera felt a pang of sympathy but reminded herself of the warnings. "What can I do to set you free?"

The spirit hesitated, its form flickering. "Break the binding seal at the base of the tree," it said. "But beware—the seal holds my power as well. If broken carelessly, it could destroy more than just me."

Kabir stepped in. "It's a trick. Spirits like this will say anything to escape. You must complete the ritual to banish it."

Meera looked between Kabir and the spirit, torn. "What if it's telling the truth? What if it just wants peace?"

Chapter 7: Crossing the Threshold

Meera decided to trust her instincts. She stepped closer to the base of the tree, ignoring Kabir's protests. The seal was a faint, glowing symbol etched into the wood, pulsing faintly with an otherworldly light. Meera touched it, and a surge of energy shot through her, showing her glimpses of the spirit's past.

She saw a powerful tantrik, revered and feared by the villagers, performing rituals beneath the banyan tree. The tantrik's ambition had drawn the ire of his peers, who conspired to trap him in his own spell, binding his soul to the tree. Over the centuries, the spirit had grown bitter, its power corrupted by anger and isolation.

Meera's vision ended as she pulled her hand away. "It was betrayed," she said, turning to Kabir. "We can't just banish it. We have to release it properly."

Kabir hesitated but nodded. "Then we'll need to modify the ritual. Follow my lead."

Together, they chanted a new incantation, one that combined the diary's instructions with prayers for liberation. The spirit writhed and howled, its form shifting between monstrous and human. The air crackled with energy as the seal began to dissolve.

Chapter 8: The Battle of Wills

The spirit resisted, its rage boiling over. "You cannot undo centuries of pain so easily!" it roared, sending waves of dark energy toward the circle. The protective boundary held, but cracks began to appear in the ground around them.

Meera focused on the talisman, channeling her will into it. "You don't have to suffer anymore," she said, her voice steady despite the chaos. "Let go of your anger. Find peace."

The spirit's form flickered, its glowing eyes dimming. For a moment, it seemed to consider her words. But as the final traces of the seal faded, a burst of energy erupted from the tree, throwing Meera and Kabir to the ground.

When the dust settled, the spirit's form had changed. It no longer looked monstrous but appeared as a weary, sorrowful figure. "Thank you," it said softly, before dissolving into the night.

Chapter 9: The Release

The banyan tree stood silent, its malevolence gone. Meera and Kabir sat in the clearing, exhausted but relieved. The air felt lighter, and the oppressive energy that had surrounded the tree was no more.

"You did it," Kabir said, a faint smile on his face. "You set it free."

Meera nodded, her hands still clutching the talisman. "I think it just needed someone to listen."

As dawn broke, they returned to the house, where Dadi awaited them with a mixture of relief and concern. "The tree's power is gone," she said, peering out at the backyard. "You've done what no one else could."

Chapter 10: A New Dawn

Life in Ranikhet slowly returned to normal. The banyan tree remained, but it no longer cast an ominous shadow over the house. Birds nested in its branches, and children played beneath it, unaware of the darkness that had once lingered there.

Kabir left the town, promising to return if ever needed. Meera, meanwhile, felt a newfound sense of purpose. The experience had changed her, teaching her the value of courage and compassion.

As she stood beneath the banyan tree one evening, she whispered a quiet thank-you to the spirit. The wind rustled the leaves, almost as if it were answering her. Meera smiled, knowing that she had not only freed the spirit but also herself from the fears that had once held her back.

CHAPTER TWO

Reflections of the Past

Chapter 1: The Antique Store

In the bustling city of Jaipur, amidst the vibrant bazaars and ancient forts, there was a little-known antique shop tucked away in a narrow alley. Kavya, a 21-year-old university student with a passion for history, often wandered into such places, searching for treasures from the past. On one such visit, she stumbled upon a peculiar item: a large, ornate mirror with an intricately carved wooden frame that seemed to whisper secrets from another era.

"How much for this?" she asked the shopkeeper, an elderly man with a knowing smile.

"That mirror, beta, comes with a story," he replied. "It's said to be cursed. Are you sure you want it?"

Kavya rolled her eyes. "You're just trying to make it more intriguing. How much?"

After some bargaining, she purchased the mirror and had it delivered to her small apartment near her college. Little did she know, she had just invited a fragment of the past into her life.

Kavya spent the rest of the day rearranging her room to accommodate the mirror. She admired its intricate carvings, running her fingers over the delicate floral patterns. Despite the shopkeeper's warning, she felt a strange connection to it, as if it had been waiting for her.

Chapter 2: The First Glimpse

Kavya hung the mirror in her bedroom, admiring how it seemed to give the room a vintage charm. That night, as she lay in bed scrolling through her phone, she thought she saw movement in the mirror from the corner of her eye. She dismissed it as a trick of the light and went to sleep.

Over the next few days, strange occurrences began to unfold. Objects in her room seemed to shift positions, and she often felt an icy chill whenever she stood near the mirror. One evening, while brushing her hair, she noticed a faint shadow behind her reflection. When she turned around, the room was empty.

On the fourth night, Kavya woke up suddenly, her heart racing. The room was eerily silent, and the air felt thick. As her eyes adjusted to the darkness, she noticed the mirror glowing faintly. She approached it cautiously, her breath hitching as she saw a pair of eyes staring back at her—eyes that weren't her own.

The unease grew stronger, but Kavya, ever the rationalist, convinced herself it was all in her head. She decided to cover the mirror with a cloth the next day, hoping to rid herself of the strange sensations.

Chapter 3: The Whisper

A week after bringing the mirror home, Kavya heard the first whisper. It was late at night, and the city was quiet. She had been studying for an upcoming exam when a soft, indistinct voice called her name.

"Kavya..."

She froze, her pen slipping from her fingers. The voice seemed to come from the mirror. Summoning her courage, she approached it and stared into her reflection. For a moment, everything seemed normal. But as she turned away, the whisper came again, louder this time.

Her heart raced as she pulled a bedsheet over the mirror, hoping to block whatever presence was haunting her. That night, her dreams were filled with fragmented images of a woman dressed in old-fashioned clothing, her eyes filled with sorrow.

Kavya awoke drenched in sweat, the woman's face etched into her mind. She decided it was time to dig deeper into the mirror's history.

Chapter 4: The Hidden Past

Determined to uncover the truth, Kavya began researching the mirror's origins. She visited the antique shop again, but the shopkeeper was reluctant to speak. "That mirror has been in my family for generations," he finally admitted. "It's said to belong to a woman named Amara, who lived during the early 19th century. They say she died tragically, but no one knows how."

Kavya's curiosity deepened. She searched archives and libraries, piecing together Amara's story. Amara was a courtesan in the royal court, known for her beauty and grace. She had fallen in love with a prince, but their love was forbidden. Betrayed by someone she trusted, Amara was accused of treason and executed in front of the very mirror that now hung in Kavya's room.

The details were chilling. Kavya couldn't shake the feeling that Amara's spirit was reaching out to her for help.

Chapter 5: The Connection

That night, Kavya's dreams were more vivid than ever. She found herself standing in a grand hall filled with candlelight, wearing a dress that wasn't hers. In the mirror, she saw not her own reflection but Amara's.

"Help me," Amara's voice echoed in the dream. "I'm trapped."

Kavya woke up in a cold sweat, the whisper from the mirror lingering in her ears. The pieces were falling into place: Amara's soul was bound to the mirror, reliving her tragic fate. But why had it chosen Kavya?

Over the following days, the visions became more frequent. Kavya saw glimpses of Amara's life—her love, her betrayal, and her despair. It became clear that the mirror was not just a relic of the past but a prison for a tormented soul.

Chapter 6: The Warning

The next day, Kavya's best friend, Rohan, visited her apartment. She confided in him about the strange events. Rohan, skeptical at first, agreed to stay the night and keep watch.

At midnight, as they sat in the living room, the temperature dropped sharply. The covered mirror began to shake violently. Rohan pulled the sheet away, revealing Amara's anguished face staring back at them."She's trying to warn you," Rohan said, his voice trembling. "But about what?"

The room grew colder, and the reflection began to change, showing images of a man—Amara's betrayer. His face was twisted with malice, his laughter echoing in the room. Kavya and Rohan realized that the mirror was not only a window to the past but also a battleground for unresolved conflict.

Chapter 7: The Ritual

Kavya's research led her to a local pandit who specialized in cleansing rituals. He explained that Amara's soul could only be freed by confronting her past. The ritual required Kavya to recreate the night of Amara's death, using the mirror as a portal.

On the appointed night, Kavya, Rohan, and the pandit prepared for the ritual. They placed candles around the mirror and began chanting sacred mantras. The mirror's surface rippled like water, and the room filled with the scent of jasmine—Amara's favorite flower.

As the ritual progressed, the room became a vortex of light and shadow. Kavya felt herself being pulled into the mirror, her surroundings dissolving into darkness.

Chapter 8: The Truth Revealed

Kavya found herself in the royal court, witnessing the events that led to Amara's death. She saw the betrayal, the false accusations, and the moment Amara was condemned.

But something was amiss. In the vision, Kavya noticed a man—one of Amara's trusted confidants—whispering to the king. He was the true traitor, framing Amara to save himself.

Amara turned to Kavya in the vision. "Expose the truth. Only then will I be free."

Kavya confronted the man in the vision, calling out his betrayal. The scene shifted, and the mirror's glow intensified. Amara's spirit began to rise, her chains breaking one by one.

Chapter 9: The Final Confrontation

Kavya returned to reality, determined to help Amara. She placed a hand on the mirror, channeling her intent. "You were wronged," she said. "Let your story be known."

The mirror glowed brightly, and Amara's spirit emerged, confronting the shadow of the man who had betrayed her. The room shook as their energies clashed, but Amara's will proved stronger. With a final cry, the betrayer's shadow dissolved, and Amara's face softened.

"Thank you," she said, her form fading. "I'm free now."

Chapter 10: A New Beginning

The mirror returned to its ordinary state, its surface now smooth and unremarkable. Kavya and Rohan watched as the room returned to normal, the oppressive atmosphere lifted.

Kavya decided to donate the mirror to a museum, ensuring Amara's story would be remembered. Life moved on, but Kavya was forever changed by the experience. She had not only uncovered a forgotten history but had also learned the power of compassion and courage.

As she walked through the bustling streets of Jaipur, the world seemed brighter, the past no longer a shadow but a lesson etched in time.

CHAPTER THREE

Shadows of the Orphanage

Chapter 1: The Arrival

Ananya was sixteen when she first laid eyes on the imposing structure of St. Mark's Orphanage. Perched on a lonely hill outside Shimla, the building seemed like a relic from another era. Its stone facade was covered in ivy, and the windows were dark, reflecting the overcast sky. As her father's car pulled into the gravel driveway, she felt a shiver run down her spine.

"This place looks like it's out of a horror movie," Ananya muttered.

Her father sighed. "It's just for a few weeks. Your mother and I need to finalize some arrangements. Besides, it'll be good for you to spend time with the other kids."

Ananya didn't reply. She stared at the wrought-iron gates, noticing how the paint had peeled away to reveal rust. As they approached the main entrance, an elderly woman in a faded blue sari greeted them.

"Welcome to St. Mark's," the woman said. Her voice was kind, but her eyes held a trace of sadness. "I'm Sister Agnes.

You must be Ananya."

Ananya nodded reluctantly. Sister Agnes led them inside, where the air smelled faintly of damp wood and mothballs. The hallways were lined with portraits of stern-looking men and women, their eyes following her as she walked past.

"Your room is upstairs," Sister Agnes said. "I'll show you around after you've settled in."

As Ananya climbed the creaking staircase, she couldn't shake the feeling that she was being watched.

Chapter 2: The Whispers

The first night in the orphanage was eerily quiet. Ananya's room was small, with a single bed, a wooden wardrobe, and a window overlooking the dense forest that surrounded the hill. She lay awake, staring at the ceiling, listening to the occasional creak of the old building.

Around midnight, she heard it: a faint whisper, almost like a child's voice, coming from the hallway. She sat up, her heart pounding.

"Hello?" she called out.

The whispering stopped. Gathering her courage, Ananya got out of bed and opened the door. The hallway was dark, lit only by the moonlight streaming through the windows. She saw nothing unusual, but the whispers started again, softer this time, as if they were coming from the walls themselves.

She shut the door quickly and climbed back into bed, pulling the blanket over her head. Sleep didn't come easily that night.

Chapter 3: The Stories

The next morning, Ananya joined the other children in the dining hall. There were about twenty of them, ranging in age from toddlers to teenagers. Most of them seemed cheerful, but Ananya noticed a few sitting quietly in the corners, their eyes downcast.

At breakfast, she struck up a conversation with a boy named Rishi. He was around her age, with a mop of curly hair and a mischievous grin.

"So, what's the deal with this place?" Ananya asked, keeping her voice low.

Rishi glanced around before leaning in. "You mean the whispers?"

Ananya's eyes widened. "You hear them too?"

"Everyone does," Rishi said. "This orphanage has a history. They say it's haunted by the children who used to live here."

"What happened to them?"

Rishi hesitated. "Some say they disappeared. Others think..." He trailed off, his expression darkening. "Just don't wander around at night."

Chapter 4: The Locked Room

Ananya couldn't ignore her curiosity. That evening, while everyone else was busy with chores, she decided to explore the orphanage. She roamed the hallways, her footsteps echoing against the stone floors. Most of the doors were unlocked, revealing dusty storage rooms and unused bedrooms. But one door at the end of a corridor was bolted shut.

She tried the handle, but it wouldn't budge. Just as she was about to leave, she heard a faint sound from the other side—a soft tapping, like fingers drumming against wood. "Who's there?" she whispered. The tapping stopped. Ananya's pulse quickened. She leaned closer, pressing her ear against the door. A chill ran through her as she heard the faint sound of a child's laughter.

Chapter 5: The Journal

Over the next few days, Ananya couldn't stop thinking about the locked room. She decided to dig deeper. One afternoon, while helping Sister Agnes organize the library, she stumbled upon an old leather-bound journal tucked away on a dusty shelf. The cover was embossed with the initials "E.M."

Curious, Ananya opened it. The pages were filled with neat handwriting, chronicling the daily life of a girl named Eliza who had lived in the orphanage decades ago. As Ananya read, she discovered entries about strange occurrences—objects moving on their own, shadows that didn't belong, and a mysterious figure that appeared in the mirrors at night.

The final entry sent a shiver down her spine:

"They're coming for me. I can hear them in the walls. If anyone finds this, please remember me."

Chapter 6: The Shadows

That night, Ananya's dreams were filled with unsettling images—a girl with hollow eyes, wandering the orphanage, her pale hands reaching out for help. When she woke up, the whispers were louder than ever, accompanied by the sound of footsteps pacing outside her door.

She mustered the courage to look outside, but the hallway was empty. As she turned back, she caught a glimpse of a shadow darting across her room. It wasn't hers.

Chapter 7: The Discovery

Determined to uncover the truth, Ananya enlisted Rishi's help. Together, they searched the orphanage for clues. In the basement, they found an old, rusted chest. Inside were photographs of children, including Eliza, and a faded newspaper clipping about a fire that had destroyed part of the orphanage years ago.

"Several children went missing after the fire," the article read. "Their bodies were never found."

Chapter 8: The Confrontation

The whispers reached a crescendo that night. Ananya and Rishi decided to confront whatever was haunting the orphanage. Armed with flashlights and the journal, they made their way to the locked room. To their surprise, the door was ajar.

Inside, the room was icy cold. At the center stood a mirror, its surface rippling like water. As they approached, shadows began to emerge from the glass—children, their faces pale and eyes hollow.

"Help us," they whispered in unison.

Chapter 9: The Sacrifice

Ananya realized that the mirror was a portal, trapping the souls of the lost children. To free them, she would have to break it. But as she raised a heavy candlestick to shatter the glass, a dark figure emerged, its voice echoing through the room.

"You cannot save them," it hissed. "They belong to me."

Summoning all her courage, Ananya swung the candlestick. The mirror shattered, releasing a blinding light. The figure let out an unearthly scream as it dissolved into the darkness.

Chapter 10: The Aftermath

The orphanage felt different the next morning—lighter, as if a heavy weight had been lifted. The whispers were gone, and the air no longer felt oppressive. Ananya and Rishi shared a quiet moment in the garden, reflecting on what they had experienced.

Sister Agnes approached them, her eyes moist with gratitude. "You've done something incredible," she said. "They're finally at peace."

As Ananya left St. Mark's a week later, she glanced back at the building one last time. For the first time, it didn't seem so foreboding. She felt a sense of closure, knowing that the shadows were gone.

CHAPTER FOUR

The Forest of Shadows

Chapter 1: The Forbidden Path

Nestled on the outskirts of Manali was the small village of Devgarh, surrounded by dense forests that seemed to whisper ancient secrets. Every villager knew of the Forbidden Path, a trail that cut through the heart of the forest. Elders warned their children, "Stay away from the path. It leads to nothing but darkness."

Arjun, a 22-year-old adventurer from Mumbai, arrived in Devgarh on a break from his studies. He had heard tales of the forest but dismissed them as superstitions. When he stumbled upon the trail during an evening walk, curiosity got the better of him.

"How dangerous can a path be?" he muttered to himself. He stepped onto the trail, unaware that he had just entered a realm where light and shadow danced to the tune of ancient spirits.

Chapter 2: The Shadow Figures

The forest seemed alive as Arjun ventured deeper. The air grew colder, and the canopy above thickened, blocking out the sun. He noticed odd carvings on the trees—symbols he couldn't recognize. The sound of rustling leaves followed him, though there was no breeze.

Then he saw them: shadowy figures flitting between the trees. At first, he thought they were tricks of the light, but as they drew closer, he realized they had no faces, just dark, shifting forms.

Panic set in, and Arjun turned to leave. But the path behind him had vanished, replaced by an unending wall of trees. The figures circled him, their whispers growing louder. "Why have you come?" they murmured.

Chapter 3: The Hermit

Just as Arjun felt his courage falter, a flickering light appeared in the distance. He ran toward it, stumbling into a clearing where an old hermit sat by a fire. The man's eyes were sharp despite his weathered face.

"You've angered the forest," the hermit said without looking up. "It does not take kindly to intruders."

"I didn't mean to," Arjun stammered. "I didn't know."

The hermit handed him a pouch filled with a pungent powder. "This will protect you for a while. But if you want to leave, you must make amends. Find the altar and offer what you value most."

Before Arjun could ask more, the hermit vanished, leaving behind only the fire, which extinguished itself moments later.

Chapter 4: The Altar of Sacrifice

Arjun continued along the trail, clutching the pouch tightly. The shadow figures kept their distance but didn't disappear. After what felt like hours, he stumbled upon an ancient stone altar covered in moss and vines. Strange symbols were etched into its surface, glowing faintly in the dark.

As he approached, the whispers returned. "What will you give?" they asked.

Arjun hesitated. What did he have to offer? He emptied his pockets: a wallet, a phone, a family photo. The shadows remained silent until he placed the photo on the altar. The symbols glowed brighter, and the photo disintegrated into ash. The shadows receded, leaving a narrow path open before him.

Chapter 5: The Guardian's Warning

The path led Arjun to a small pond, its surface eerily still. As he knelt to drink, a voice spoke. "You shouldn't have come here."

Startled, Arjun looked up to see a woman standing on the other side of the pond. Her eyes glowed faintly, and her presence radiated an unnatural aura.

"Who are you?" he asked.

"I am the Guardian," she replied. "This forest was once a sanctuary, but it's been cursed by those who sought to exploit its power. Now, it traps all who enter. If you wish to leave, you must lift the curse."

She explained that the curse was tied to a relic hidden deep within the forest. Destroying it would set the spirits free, but the journey would be perilous.

Chapter 6: The Relic's Curse

Arjun's search for the relic led him through treacherous terrain. The forest seemed determined to stop him—trees shifted to block his path, roots tried to trip him, and the shadow figures grew bolder, their whispers turning to screams.

Eventually, he found the relic: a blackened, twisted idol resting in a grove of dead trees. The air around it felt heavy, suffocating. As he reached for it, the shadows converged, forming a monstrous entity with glowing red eyes.

"Leave," it bellowed. "This is not your fight."

But Arjun remembered the Guardian's words. Summoning his courage, he hurled the pouch of powder at the entity. The shadows recoiled, giving him just enough time to grab the idol and smash it against a rock.

Chapter 7: The Forest's Wrath

The ground shook as the idol shattered, releasing a burst of dark energy. The shadow entity let out a deafening roar before disintegrating into nothingness. The forest seemed to come alive with rage—trees swayed violently, and the wind howled like a wounded animal.

Arjun ran, dodging falling branches and uprooted trees. The path reappeared before him, and he sprinted toward the light at its end. Just as he reached the edge of the forest, a familiar voice stopped him.

"Thank you," the Guardian said, her figure appearing briefly among the trees. "The forest remembers."

Chapter 8: The Return

When Arjun emerged from the forest, the sun was rising, casting a warm glow over Devgarh. He stumbled into the village, where the elders greeted him with a mix of astonishment and relief.

"You survived," one of them said. "The forest has spared you. It must mean the curse is lifted."

Arjun didn't stay to explain. He returned to his room, exhausted but alive. That night, his dreams were filled with images of the forest, the Guardian, and the shadows. When he woke, he felt a strange sense of peace.

Chapter 9: The Forest's Gift

A week later, Arjun prepared to leave Devgarh. As he packed, he found a small token in his bag: a wooden carving of the Guardian. It was intricately detailed, and he knew it hadn't been there before.

He took it as a sign of gratitude from the forest. Though he was glad to leave, a part of him felt drawn to return one day.

Chapter 10: The Legend Lives On

Years later, stories of the Forest of Shadows began to change. The villagers spoke of how the darkness had lifted, though the Forbidden Path remained a place of mystery. Travelers who ventured near claimed to feel a watchful presence, as if the forest was protecting them.

As for Arjun, he kept the carving on his desk as a reminder of his journey. He often wondered if the Guardian still watched over the forest, ensuring its secrets remained safe.

And somewhere deep within the woods, the shadows stirred, waiting for the next soul brave enough to enter.

CHAPTER FIVE

Whispers of the Well

Chapter 1: The Forgotten Village

Deep in the heart of Madhya Pradesh lay the abandoned village of Khandara, shrouded in mystery and overgrown with wild vegetation. Once a bustling settlement, it was now nothing more than crumbling ruins. The locals of nearby villages avoided the place, whispering tales of a cursed well that consumed anyone who dared approach.

Ishaan, a 23-year-old journalist and aspiring documentarian, was drawn to such tales. His YouTube channel, *India Uncovered*, was steadily gaining traction, and the legend of Khandara seemed like the perfect story to captivate his audience. Accompanied by his best friends, Meera and Aditya, he decided to visit the forgotten village to uncover the truth behind the whispers.

"Are you sure about this?" Meera asked as they stood at the edge of the forest that concealed Khandara.

Ishaan grinned. "Come on, Meera. It's just an old village. What's the worst that could happen?"

But as they stepped into the forest, a chilling wind swept through, carrying with it the faint sound of whispers.

Chapter 2: The Silent Arrival

The trio reached the village by late afternoon. The setting sun cast long shadows over the desolate streets. Stone houses with collapsed roofs and moss-covered walls stood as silent witnesses to the passage of time. At the center of the village was the well, surrounded by a low, broken stone wall and covered with a rusted iron grate.

"That must be it," Ishaan said, setting up his camera. The well's presence was almost magnetic, drawing their attention despite the growing unease in the air.

Aditya peered over the edge, his flashlight illuminating the dark abyss below. "It's deeper than I thought."

"Let's get some shots before it gets too dark," Ishaan suggested.

As they filmed, the whispers grew louder. They dismissed them as the sound of the wind—but deep down, each of them felt a creeping dread.

Chapter 3: The First Night

Unable to leave the forest safely after sundown, the group decided to camp in one of the intact houses. They built a fire and tried to make light of the situation, but the atmosphere was oppressive.

In the dead of night, Meera was awoken by the sound of soft sobbing. She looked around and saw Ishaan and Aditya fast asleep. The sound seemed to come from outside. Against her better judgment, she stepped out of the house.

The sobbing grew louder as she approached the well. Suddenly, it stopped. A faint voice whispered her name: "Meera..."

Terrified, she ran back inside, locking the door behind her. The others woke to her trembling form, but she refused to tell them what had happened, fearing they'd think she was imagining things.

Chapter 4: Unearthing the Legend

The next morning, Ishaan decided to interview a local elder for more information about the well. They visited a nearby village and met Dadi Sita, a woman in her eighties who was reluctant to speak at first. But when Ishaan mentioned the well, her expression darkened.

"That well is cursed," she said. "Many years ago, a young girl named Chaya lived in Khandara. She was accused of witchcraft when crops failed and livestock died. The villagers threw her into the well, believing it would break the curse."

"And?" Ishaan asked, leaning forward.

"She didn't die immediately," Dadi Sita said. "Her screams echoed for days. When the villagers returned to check, they found the well's water had turned black. Since then, anyone who approaches it hears her voice, and some are never seen again."

Chapter 5: The Unseen Force

That evening, back in Khandara, the trio reviewed their footage. As they watched the clips of the well, strange anomalies appeared on the screen—shadows darting past, shapes forming in the darkness.

"This is incredible," Ishaan said, though his enthusiasm was tinged with fear.

Aditya wasn't convinced. "It could just be a glitch."

"What about the whispers?" Meera asked. "You heard them too, right?"

Before anyone could answer, the fire they had built flickered violently and went out. The room plunged into darkness, and the whispers returned, louder and more insistent.

Chapter 6: The Descent

Determined to uncover the truth, Ishaan suggested they lower a camera into the well. Despite Meera's protests, Aditya agreed to help.

They secured the camera to a rope and slowly lowered it into the well. The screen showed the stone walls descending endlessly. Suddenly, the camera's light illuminated something unnatural—a pale, emaciated figure clinging to the wall.

Before they could react, the rope was yanked violently, pulling the camera into the darkness. A blood-curdling scream erupted from the well, sending the trio stumbling back.

Chapter 7: The Mark

The next morning, Ishaan woke up with strange marks on his arms—thin, red scratches that resembled claw marks. Meera noticed similar marks on her own wrists.

"We need to leave," she insisted. "This isn't worth it."

But Ishaan was determined. "If we leave now, we'll never know the truth. We're so close."

Reluctantly, Meera and Aditya agreed to stay one more night. They decided to conduct a final investigation at the well, hoping to find answers.

Chapter 8: The Spirit's Tale

As darkness fell, they gathered around the well, lighting candles to keep the shadows at bay. Meera, who had grown increasingly empathetic toward Chaya, spoke softly.

"We're not here to hurt you," she said. "Tell us what you want."

The whispers subsided, replaced by a single voice. "Justice."

A vision overtook them, showing the villagers' cruelty toward Chaya. They saw her thrown into the well, begging for mercy. Her anguish turned to rage as she cursed the village with her dying breath.

Chapter 9: The Ritual

The group realized that the only way to appease Chaya's spirit was to perform a ritual to honor her and acknowledge her suffering. They retrieved offerings from the village—flowers, food, and a diya lamp.

As they placed the items around the well and lit the lamp, the air grew still. Chaya's spirit emerged, her face no longer twisted with anger but filled with sorrow.

"Thank you," she whispered. "The curse is lifted."

Her form dissolved into the night, and the oppressive energy around the well dissipated.

Chapter 10: The Aftermath

The trio left Khandara the next morning, the village no longer shrouded in darkness. Ishaan uploaded their footage, but some parts—the most supernatural—were inexplicably corrupted.

Though they had lifted the curse, the experience stayed with them. Meera often dreamed of Chaya, while Ishaan received messages from viewers claiming to hear whispers in his videos.

Khandara's story became legend, a tale of justice, redemption, and the lingering power of the past.

CHAPTER SIX

The Haunting of Saraighat Bridge

Chapter 1: Arrival in Guwahati

The sprawling city of Guwahati welcomed Ananya Roy with open arms, its vibrant chaos both overwhelming and invigorating. As a budding journalist for a digital magazine specializing in folklore and urban legends, Ananya had carved a niche exploring tales that blurred the line between reality and myth. Her latest assignment had brought her to Assam to investigate one of the region's most spine-chilling legends—the haunting of Saraighat Bridge.

Standing on the banks of the mighty Brahmaputra River, Ananya gazed at the bridge that stretched across its expanse, a marvel of mid-20th-century engineering. Built between 1959 and 1962, the Saraighat Bridge was a lifeline connecting Assam's two halves. However, its history was shrouded in tragedy. Tales of construction workers plunging to their deaths into the river's unforgiving currents, unexplained malfunctions, and spectral figures roaming its steel framework intrigued Ananya.

She had heard whispers of this legend from a local contact, Nayan, who worked as a guide. "The spirits don't rest," Nayan had warned her as they sipped tea in a bustling Guwahati cafe. "Many lost their lives building that bridge. Their cries still echo at night."

Determined to uncover the truth, Ananya booked a small guesthouse near the river. That night, as she lay in her room, the rhythmic murmur of the Brahmaputra seemed to carry voices, faint but persistent. Sleep came only after a restless battle with her curiosity.

Chapter 2: The First Encounter

The next morning, armed with her camera and notebook, Ananya ventured to the bridge. As sunlight danced on the river's surface, the bridge seemed like any other. Yet, beneath its steel and concrete façade, there was an undeniable air of melancholy.

She spent hours interviewing locals. Vendors who sold tea and snacks to passersby were reluctant to speak of the hauntings. "At night, strange things happen," an elderly tea seller finally confided. "Shadowy figures, sudden chills... the bridge is alive with something we don't understand."

As dusk settled, Ananya decided to walk across the bridge. Halfway through, her footsteps faltered. The air grew heavier, and a faint metallic clang echoed, as though someone unseen was hammering the girders. Her breath quickened when she spotted a silhouette ahead. It stood motionless, blocking her path. Ananya's voice trembled as she called out, "Hello? Is someone there?"

The figure turned, and she gasped. Its face was featureless, shrouded in shadow, yet its form was unmistakably human. Before she could react, it vanished.

Heart pounding, Ananya stumbled back toward the city.

Chapter 3: A Town's Silent Secret

The next day, Ananya sought answers. Nayan agreed to accompany her to the Assam State Archives, where they unearthed reports of the bridge's construction. Yellowed newspaper clippings revealed stories of accidents and mysterious disappearances. At least 23 workers had reportedly fallen to their deaths, their bodies claimed by the Brahmaputra's depths. Rumors of faulty equipment and unsafe working conditions had been swept under the rug, overshadowed by the bridge's successful completion.

"It's no wonder the spirits linger," Nayan remarked grimly. "Their deaths were ignored, their sacrifices forgotten."

An elderly librarian overheard their conversation and hesitantly approached. "The hauntings are real," she whispered. "My grandfather worked on that bridge. He spoke of hearing cries in the night, even during construction. Some said the river itself was angry."

Ananya's resolve deepened. She needed to experience the bridge at its most active—during the stillness of night.

Chapter 4: Night on the Bridge

That evening, Ananya prepared for a long vigil. She packed her camera, voice recorder, and a thermos of coffee, determined to document any unusual activity. By midnight, the city had quieted, and the bridge loomed under a pale moon.

The first hour was uneventful, save for the occasional passing vehicle. But as the night deepened, the atmosphere shifted. A sudden chill crept over Ananya, and the surrounding silence grew oppressive. Her camera captured faint orbs of light darting along the bridge's length, though no source was visible.

Then, a chilling cry pierced the night. It was faint, like a lament carried on the wind, but unmistakable. Ananya gripped her recorder, her fingers trembling. "If anyone is here," she called out, "please show yourself."

The bridge responded with a groan, the metal beneath her feet vibrating. A distant figure appeared, slowly approaching. Ananya's courage faltered, but she stood her ground. As the figure drew near, she realized it wore a worker's uniform, soaked and torn. Its hollow eyes locked onto hers before it dissolved into mist.

Chapter 5: The Brahmaputra's Depths

Shaken but determined, Ananya sought out a local fisherman, Anil, who had worked the Brahmaputra's waters for decades. Over a cup of steaming chai, he recounted his own encounters in vivid detail.

"I've pulled up helmets and tools from the river," Anil said, his voice heavy. "But sometimes, I find other things—things that shouldn't be there. Once, I felt a hand grab my net. When I looked, there was nothing but water."

He gestured toward the bridge. "They're still down there, you know. The river doesn't give up its dead so easily."

Ananya's curiosity deepened as Anil shared more eerie tales. "I've heard voices—angry voices—calling from below. It's like they want something, but I don't know what."

Ananya asked if he would take her onto the river that night. Anil hesitated but eventually agreed, warning her of the risks.

Chapter 6: The River's Secrets

On a moonlit night, Ananya and Anil ventured onto the Brahmaputra in a small boat. The river's surface glistened, but its depths felt ominous. As they neared the bridge, the temperature dropped sharply, and the boat's motor sputtered before cutting out entirely.

"Not again," Anil muttered, reaching for the oars.

Suddenly, the water around them churned violently. A faint glow emanated from beneath the surface, forming the outline of hands reaching upward. Ananya's breath caught as spectral figures emerged, their faces twisted in anguish.

"They're asking for justice," Anil whispered. "They want to be remembered."

Ananya leaned closer to the water, feeling a powerful pull. "We need to help them," she said softly. "But how?"

Chapter 7: The Spirit's Warning

Back on land, Ananya pieced together the story. The spirits were bound by their untimely deaths, seeking acknowledgment and closure. She delved into old records and discovered discrepancies in the bridge's construction reports. Corners had been cut, and lives had been sacrificed for expediency.

That night, Ananya had a vivid dream. A spectral worker appeared, his voice echoing in her mind: "Tell our story. Only then will we find peace."

The dream continued with haunting images of the construction site—the chaos, the fear, the final moments of the workers. Ananya woke up drenched in sweat, but more determined than ever.

Chapter 8: A Ritual of Remembrance

With the help of a local priest, Ananya organized a memorial service on the bridge. Candles were lit, prayers were offered, and the names of the lost workers were read aloud. The air grew lighter, and the bridge seemed to sigh with relief.

The ceremony was attended by locals, some of whom shared their own eerie experiences. Ananya felt a sense of accomplishment but knew her work wasn't over.

Chapter 9: Closure (or Not?)

In the following days, reports of hauntings diminished. The bridge, once a place of fear, became a site of quiet reverence. Ananya returned to her magazine with a story that resonated deeply with readers. Her article became a sensation, drawing attention to the forgotten history of the Saraighat Bridge and its workers.

Chapter 10: The Haunting Never Ends

Months later, Ananya received an anonymous letter. Inside was a photo of the bridge, with a shadowy figure standing at its center. Below it, a note read: "Not all stories end."

CHAPTER SEVEN

The Whispering Shadows

Chapter 1: The Arrival at Whispering Pines

Nine-year-old Aarav clutched his toy train tightly as the car rumbled up the winding road. His parents, Ramesh and Priya, had decided to escape the bustling city of Delhi for a peaceful summer in a quaint hill town called Whispering Pines. The town, nestled amidst dense forests and rolling hills, seemed idyllic. Aarav wasn't convinced. The large colonial-style house they were renting felt old and eerie. Its wooden beams creaked, and its windows rattled with the faintest breeze.

"This house is over a hundred years old," the caretaker, Mr. Das, had informed them. "Built by the British, it's seen many stories."

That night, as Aarav lay in his room staring at the high ceiling, he heard a faint whisper. It wasn't the rustling of leaves or the call of nocturnal creatures. It was a voice. A child's voice.

"Come play with me..."

Aarav sat up, his heart racing. He looked around but saw nothing. Clutching his toy tighter, he convinced himself it was just his imagination. Yet, deep down, he wasn't sure.

Chapter 2: The First Encounter

The next morning, Aarav explored the sprawling grounds of Whispering Pines. The backyard led to a dense forest, where tall pine trees swayed in the cool breeze. Priya warned him not to wander too far, but Aarav's curiosity got the better of him.

As he ventured deeper, he came across a small clearing. In its center stood a crumbling stone well, covered in moss. The air felt colder here, and Aarav's toy train slipped from his grasp as he heard the voice again.

"Play with me," it whispered, louder this time.

Aarav spun around and saw a figure—a girl about his age. She wore an old-fashioned white dress and had long, unkempt hair. Her pale face bore a faint smile.

"Who are you?" Aarav asked, his voice trembling.

"My name is Lily," she said softly. "Do you want to play hide and seek?"

Before Aarav could respond, she turned and ran into the forest. Against his better judgment, he followed.

Chapter 3: Secrets of the Well

Lily was fast. Aarav struggled to keep up as she darted through the trees. Suddenly, she stopped near the well and pointed toward it.

"It's in there," she said cryptically.

"What is?" Aarav asked, peering into the darkness of the well.

Before Lily could answer, Priya's voice echoed through the forest, calling Aarav's name. He turned to look, and when he looked back, Lily was gone.

At dinner that evening, Aarav told his parents about the girl. Ramesh chuckled. "Maybe she's a local kid. The caretaker mentioned some families live near the forest."

But Mr. Das's expression darkened when Aarav mentioned Lily. "There hasn't been a family with a child named Lily here for decades," he said. "You must be mistaken."

Chapter 4: The Old Diary

Unable to shake the encounter, Aarav decided to investigate. While rummaging through an old chest in the attic, he discovered a leather-bound diary. The name "Lily" was etched on its cover.

The diary revealed a tragic story. Lily had lived in the house during the 1940s. She had been a lonely child, often playing by herself in the forest. One day, she had fallen into the well and drowned. Her body was never recovered, and her parents left the house shortly after.

Aarav's hands trembled as he read the last entry: "I hear whispers from the well. They want me to join them..."

Chapter 5: The Whispers Grow Louder

That night, the whispers returned, louder and more insistent. Aarav tried to ignore them, but they seeped into his dreams. He saw Lily standing by the well, surrounded by shadowy figures with hollow eyes.

The next morning, Aarav confronted Mr. Das, showing him the diary. The caretaker paled. "You should have left this alone," he muttered. "Some stories are better forgotten."

But Aarav couldn't forget. He needed to help Lily. She wasn't evil; she was just lost.

Chapter 6: Descent into Darkness

Determined to bring closure, Aarav returned to the well with a flashlight and a rope. The air grew colder as he approached, and the whispers became deafening.

"Come," they urged.

Aarav lowered the flashlight into the well and gasped. The beam illuminated a pile of bones and scraps of fabric. Among them was a small white dress.

Suddenly, the rope jerked in his hands. Aarav screamed as an unseen force pulled him toward the well. He scrambled back, clutching at the ground, until the force subsided. Breathing heavily, he fled back to the house.

Chapter 7: The Priest's Advice

Priya and Ramesh, alarmed by Aarav's pale face and trembling hands, demanded an explanation. When Aarav told them everything, Ramesh contacted the local priest, Father Dominic.

Father Dominic listened intently. "Lily's soul is trapped," he explained. "And the shadows you saw? They are other restless spirits, drawn to the well's darkness. We must perform a ritual to free them."

Chapter 8: The Ritual

Under a full moon, Father Dominic led the family to the well. He chanted prayers while Aarav held a candle, its flame flickering wildly. The shadows emerged, writhing and moaning, but the priest's voice grew louder, commanding them to leave.

Lily appeared last, her expression sorrowful. "Thank you," she whispered to Aarav before dissolving into light.

The well shuddered, then fell silent. The whispers were gone.

Chapter 9: Saying Goodbye

Life at Whispering Pines returned to normal. Aarav no longer heard voices or saw figures in the forest. Before leaving, he placed the diary and his toy train near the well, a final gift for Lily.

"Goodbye," he murmured, feeling a bittersweet sense of peace.

Chapter 10: The Lingering Shadow

Months later, back in Delhi, Aarav's mother unpacked his suitcase. Tucked inside was the diary Aarav had left by the well.

As she opened it, a faint whisper echoed through the room: "Come play with me..."

CHAPTER EIGHT

The Cursed Lantern

Chapter 1: The Auction House

In a quiet corner of Kolkata, a centuries-old auction house stood, known for its peculiar collection of artifacts. Aditya Das, a 25-year-old art historian with an eye for the extraordinary, frequented this place in search of unique pieces for his private collection. One stormy evening, a new artifact caught his attention—an old brass lantern, tarnished with age and covered in intricate carvings.

The auctioneer, a bespectacled man with a gravelly voice, leaned forward. "This piece," he began, "has an unusual history. It belonged to the Zamindar of Kalyanpur, who vanished under mysterious circumstances. Rumor has it that the lantern is cursed."

Aditya's curiosity was piqued. He wasn't one to believe in curses, but the craftsmanship of the lantern was undeniable. Intricate patterns of vines and mythical creatures adorned its surface, and the handle bore what looked like ancient script.

"How much?" Aditya asked, his voice steady despite the thrill coursing through him.

"It's not just about the price, sir," the auctioneer said, a faint smirk on his lips. "Owning such an artifact comes with responsibility. Are you sure you want it?"

Aditya nodded, and after a heated round of bidding, the lantern was his. As he walked out of the auction house with his prize, the first rumble of thunder echoed ominously overhead. The lantern felt heavier than it should have, as though it carried the weight of its history.

Chapter 2: The First Flicker

Aditya placed the lantern in his study, admiring its craftsmanship under the soft glow of a desk lamp. He turned it over, tracing the carvings with his fingers, trying to decipher their meaning. Despite its age, the lantern felt warm to the touch, almost alive.

That night, as he worked late into the hours on his laptop, a faint flicker caught his attention. He glanced at the lantern, which was unlit, yet it seemed to emit a dim, eerie glow. Startled, he got up and inspected it. There was no bulb or any apparent source of light inside.

"Must be the reflection from the lamp," he muttered, though his voice wavered.

Dismissing it as his imagination, Aditya went to bed. But his dreams that night were vivid and unsettling. He saw shadowy figures moving through dense forests, the lantern's light guiding them. He woke up drenched in sweat, his heart racing. To his shock, the lantern was no longer on the study table. It sat on his bedside table, as though it had been watching him all along.

Chapter 3: The Whispering Light

Over the next few days, Aditya began to notice more oddities. The flickering glow of the lantern became more frequent, often accompanied by faint whispers. At first, he dismissed them as the hum of the city outside his apartment, but soon they grew louder, more distinct. The whispers seemed to form words, though he couldn't quite make them out.

Determined to understand its origins, Aditya dove into research. He scoured libraries, online forums, and even reached out to local historians. The story of the Zamindar of Kalyanpur unfolded before him. The Zamindar had been a tyrant, known for his greed and cruelty. He had commissioned the lantern from a skilled craftsman, claiming it would guide him through his darkest hours. But one stormy night, he vanished without a trace. The lantern was found glowing brightly in the palace, its carvings pulsing with an unearthly light.

As he delved deeper, Aditya began to feel a connection to the lantern, as though it was calling to him. The whispers grew louder at night, filling his room with an air of unease. His sleep became restless, plagued by dreams of a dark figure shrouded in mist, holding the lantern aloft.

Chapter 4: The First Encounter

One evening, unable to bear the unease alone, Aditya invited his best friend, Kavya, over to his apartment. Kavya, a freelance journalist with a knack for uncovering mysteries, was intrigued by his tales of the lantern.

As he recounted the lantern's history, Kavya moved closer to inspect it. "It's beautiful, but... unsettling," she said, her voice tinged with unease. "It feels almost... alive."

Before Aditya could respond, the lantern flared brightly, casting long, distorted shadows on the walls. The room's temperature plummeted, and a ghostly figure began to materialize in the corner. It was a tall man, his eyes glowing with malice and his expression twisted in rage. Kavya let out a scream as the figure advanced, its translucent hand reaching toward her.

Aditya grabbed the lantern instinctively, and the figure vanished, leaving behind an icy chill and the faint smell of burning. Both of them sat in silence, the gravity of what they had just witnessed sinking in.

"We need to find out what this thing wants," Kavya whispered, her hands trembling.

Chapter 5: The Curse Unveiled

Determined to uncover the truth, Aditya and Kavya embarked on a journey to Kalyanpur. The village, nestled amidst dense forests, had an air of desolation. The locals avoided eye contact, their faces etched with fear when the Zamindar's name was mentioned.

After hours of inquiries, they found an old man sitting by the ruins of the Zamindar's palace. He was thin and frail, his eyes clouded with age but sharp with knowledge. When Aditya showed him the lantern, the man's hands trembled.

"That is no ordinary lantern," he said in a hushed tone. "It's a beacon for the Zamindar's spirit. He feeds on fear and suffering. If you want to end this, you must return it to its rightful place and break the curse."

The old man handed them a faded manuscript detailing a ritual to sever the lantern's connection to the spirit. It required taking the lantern back to the palace and performing the ritual under the light of a new moon.

Chapter 6: The New Moon

On the night of the new moon, Aditya and Kavya returned to the ruins, armed with the manuscript and the lantern. The palace loomed before them, its once grand facade now a crumbling shadow of its former self. Inside, the air was thick with dust and an oppressive sense of dread.

They made their way to the central hall, where a large, cracked mirror hung on the wall. According to the manuscript, the mirror was the key to trapping the Zamindar's spirit.

As they lit the lantern, the room was bathed in an unearthly glow. The whispers grew louder, forming coherent words:

"You cannot escape me."

Chapter 7: The Spirit's Wrath

The Zamindar's spirit emerged, his form more solid and terrifying than ever. His eyes burned with rage, and his voice echoed through the hall.

"You dare defy me?" he roared, his presence causing the very walls to tremble.

Kavya began chanting the incantation from the manuscript, her voice steady despite the terror in her eyes. The spirit howled, lashing out with tendrils of shadow that shattered nearby columns. Aditya held the lantern steady, its light pulsating in response to the chant. Each pulse seemed to weaken the spirit, drawing it closer to the mirror.

Chapter 8: The Final Stand

As the chant reached its crescendo, the mirror began to crack, its surface glowing with an inner light. The Zamindar's spirit fought back, sending Kavya sprawling with a wave of energy. Aditya, clutching the manuscript, continued the chant, his voice rising above the chaos.

The lantern's glow intensified, drawing the spirit inexorably toward the mirror. With a final, deafening scream, the spirit was pulled into the glass. The mirror shattered, and the lantern's light dimmed, its curse finally broken.

Chapter 9: The Aftermath

Exhausted but alive, Aditya and Kavya stumbled out of the palace as dawn broke. They buried the shattered mirror fragments and the lantern deep within the ruins, ensuring no one would disturb them again.

Back in Kolkata, Aditya struggled to process the events. He stored the manuscript in a locked drawer, vowing never to seek out cursed artifacts again. But the experience had left an indelible mark on him, a reminder of the darkness that lurks in forgotten histories.

Chapter 10: The Lingering Shadow

Months passed, and life returned to normal. Aditya resumed his work, and Kavya moved on to new stories. But one night, as Aditya prepared for bed, he noticed a faint flicker of light in his study.

When he entered, the drawer containing the manuscript was ajar, and on his desk lay a single shard of the mirror, glowing faintly.

The whispers returned, soft but unmistakable.

"You cannot escape me."

The Haunting of Starlit Forest

Chapter 1: Arrival at the Edge

On the outskirts of a quiet village nestled in the foothills of the Himalayas lay the Starlit Forest. Known for its ethereal beauty under moonlight, the forest drew travelers and poets alike. Yet, the villagers avoided it after sunset, whispering tales of restless spirits that roamed its shadowy depths.

Rekha Sharma, an aspiring wildlife photographer, arrived in the village to document the forest's famed nocturnal creatures. Her goal was a feature for an environmental magazine, but what drew her most was the thrill of the unknown. Unbothered by the villagers' warnings, she rented a room in the modest home of an elderly woman named Amrita, whose eyes clouded with worry at Rekha's mention of night ventures into the forest.

"Starlit Forest holds secrets," Amrita warned. "Stay away after dark. The spirits there are not kind."

Rekha dismissed the warnings as local superstition. That night, she gazed at the forest's edge from her window. The towering trees seemed to pulse under the silvery glow of the moon. Somewhere deep within, she felt an almost magnetic pull. She resolved to explore the forest the next day, eager to capture its mysteries through her lens.

Chapter 2: A Flicker in the Shadows

Early the next morning, Rekha packed her camera and ventured into the forest. The sunlight filtered through the canopy, casting dappled patterns on the ground. Birds chirped, and the rustle of leaves accompanied her as she snapped photos of rare orchids and squirrels darting between branches. Every step seemed to draw her closer to something unseen yet profoundly alive.

At midday, she stumbled upon an abandoned clearing. At its center stood an old shrine, its stone walls covered in moss and cracks. Rekha's curiosity piqued when she noticed faint carvings of figures with hollow eyes and outstretched arms. The shrine seemed ancient, forgotten by time yet exuding an undeniable presence.

Suddenly, a cold wind swept through the clearing, and Rekha shivered despite the sun overhead. Her camera's lens fogged, and when she wiped it clean, she thought she saw a shadow flit across the shrine. Dismissing it as her imagination, she continued deeper into the forest. Yet, the image of the shadow lingered in her mind, gnawing at her resolve.

As evening approached, Rekha's unease grew. The forest's vibrant sounds faded, replaced by an eerie silence. When she turned back toward the village, a faint whisper seemed to follow her, too indistinct to comprehend but persistent enough to quicken her pace. She reached the safety of her room with a pounding heart and an unshakable feeling that the forest had marked her.

Chapter 3: Village Secrets

That night, Rekha shared her day's findings with Amrita. When she mentioned the shrine, the old woman's hands trembled, spilling tea onto the table.

"You should not have gone there," Amrita said, her voice hushed. "That shrine is where it began."

Rekha pressed for details, and after much hesitation, Amrita relented. Decades ago, a group of villagers sought shelter in the forest during a violent storm. When they failed to return, search parties found the shrine surrounded by unmarked graves. Since then, the forest's whispers had grown louder, and strange occurrences plagued those who ventured too far.

Determined to uncover the truth, Rekha visited the village's small library the next day. The librarian, a stooped man with glasses perched precariously on his nose, showed her old records and faded photographs. Each clue deepened the mystery, painting a picture of a forest that had long resisted human intrusion.

Chapter 4: The First Warning

As twilight descended, Rekha approached the shrine with a mix of excitement and trepidation. The air was thick, and the forest seemed alive with unseen eyes. She set up her camera, determined to capture evidence of the supernatural.

As she adjusted her tripod, a child's voice called out softly, "Help me." Rekha spun around, her flashlight beam slicing through the gloom. A faint figure stood at the edge of the clearing—a girl in a tattered dress, her face obscured by shadows.

Rekha took a cautious step forward. "Who are you? Are you lost?"

The girl pointed toward the shrine and whispered, "They're waiting." Before Rekha could respond, the figure dissolved into the air, leaving behind a faint chill. When she reviewed her camera footage later, the girl's image was missing. But the whispers were there, clearer than before, repeating a single phrase: "Don't wake them." Rekha's heart raced as she realized she was no longer just an observer in this unfolding tale—she was a participant.

Chapter 5: Into the Depths

Haunted by the encounter, Rekha returned to the village and shared her experience with a local historian, Rajiv, who had spent years studying the region's folklore. He confirmed Amrita's story but added a chilling detail—the spirits of the shrine were guardians, bound to protect something buried beneath.

"What are they protecting?" Rekha asked.

Rajiv hesitated. "Some say it's a relic. Others claim it's a curse. Whatever it is, disturbing it could unleash something far worse."

Despite the warnings, Rekha's curiosity burned brighter. She convinced Rajiv to accompany her back to the shrine the following night, hoping to uncover the truth once and for all. As they prepared their equipment, a storm gathered on the horizon, as though the forest itself anticipated their intrusion.

Chapter 6: The Unveiling

Under a blood-red moon, Rekha and Rajiv approached the shrine. Armed with a shovel and a lantern, they began digging near its base, where the carvings seemed to converge. The forest's whispers grew louder, rising to a cacophony of anguished cries.

After hours of digging, their shovel struck something hard. Unearthing it revealed a sealed urn adorned with intricate symbols. As Rekha reached out to touch it, the ground beneath them trembled, and a deafening roar echoed through the forest.

"We need to leave," Rajiv urged, but it was too late. Shadows poured from the shrine, coalescing into humanoid forms with hollow eyes. The spirits surrounded them, their mournful cries reverberating in Rekha's mind.

Chapter 7: The Forest's Wrath

The spirits' leader, a towering figure with a staff of gnarled wood, stepped forward. Its hollow voice resonated in the air. "You have disturbed our sanctuary. Leave, or face our wrath."

Rekha pleaded for forgiveness, explaining her desire to understand the forest's history. The leader's gaze bore into her, and for a moment, the spirits seemed to waver.

"Restore what you've taken," it commanded, "and swear to honor our story."

Trembling, Rekha and Rajiv reburied the urn. As they did, the forest's cries softened, replaced by an eerie silence. The spirits faded, leaving only the faint glow of the moonlight. Exhausted but relieved, they retreated to the village, vowing never to disrupt the forest again.

Chapter 8: A Village's Legacy

Back in the village, Rekha shared her experience, urging the villagers to embrace the forest's history rather than fear it. She proposed creating a memorial at the forest's edge, honoring the lives lost and the spirits that protected the land.

The villagers, moved by her passion, agreed. Together, they erected a stone marker inscribed with the forest's story, ensuring it would never be forgotten. The act seemed to soothe the forest, its once-haunting presence replaced by a serene beauty.

Chapter 9: Closure

Weeks later, Rekha published her article, complete with photographs and firsthand accounts. The story gained widespread attention, drawing visitors to the village who wished to experience the Starlit Forest's haunting beauty. Rekha's work ignited discussions about preserving folklore and respecting the natural world's mysteries.

Though the forest remained enigmatic, its whispers grew softer, as if satisfied with the newfound respect. Rekha felt a deep connection to the land, knowing she had played a part in preserving its legacy.

Chapter 10: The Whispering Shadows

One night, as Rekha prepared to leave the village, she took a final walk to the forest's edge. The trees swayed gently, their shadows dancing in the moonlight. For the first time, the whispers sounded almost welcoming.

Echoes of the Lighthouse

Chapter 1: Arrival at Velas

The Konkan coast of Maharashtra was known for its untouched beauty, dotted with golden beaches, lush mangroves, and quaint fishing villages. Ananya Dixit had always been drawn to the sea, and when her research on Olive Ridley turtles brought her to the small village of Velas, she thought she had found paradise.

Her temporary home was a modest beachside cottage, where the salty breeze carried with it the soothing rhythm of waves crashing against the shore. But the idyllic scenery came with a shadow—a towering, weather-beaten lighthouse perched on the cliffs to the north.

Kaala Rekha Lighthouse was a relic of the colonial era, its darkened bricks streaked with moss and salt. Locals avoided it, their reluctance punctuated by whispered warnings. "Don't go near the lighthouse," her landlady, Radha, had told her on her first day. "It has a dark history. The sea claims many lives, and some never leave."

Ananya, however, was not one to be deterred by local superstitions. Her scientific mind sought facts, not folklore. That evening, as she watched the lighthouse beam cut through the twilight sky from her cottage window, she felt an unexplainable pull. She decided she would visit the place soon, despite Radha's protests.

Chapter 2: Whispers on the Wind

The opportunity to visit the lighthouse came sooner than expected. While exploring the beach the next morning, she overheard two fishermen discussing it.

"It's Devak's turn to be the keeper," one said, glancing uneasily toward the cliffs. "Poor man. I wouldn't stay there a night even if I was paid a fortune."

The other nodded. "They say the spirits of the drowned sailors roam the tower. Devak's brave, but even he looks haunted these days."

Ananya approached them with polite curiosity. "What's so frightening about the lighthouse?" she asked.

The men exchanged wary looks before the older one replied, "It's cursed. The first keeper went mad and threw himself into the sea. Many others who followed either vanished or met strange deaths. They say the lighthouse calls to them—makes them jump."

Ananya suppressed a shiver. "And this Devak? Has he seen anything unusual?"

"Only he knows, but he won't talk," the younger fisherman said, shaking his head. "He's been there for three months now. That's longer than most."

The conversation intrigued Ananya even more. That afternoon, she packed her notebook and camera, determined to see the lighthouse for herself.

Chapter 3: The Keeper's Warning

The path to the lighthouse was steep and winding, bordered by dense vegetation and jagged rocks. The air grew colder as Ananya approached, the salty tang of the sea mingling with the faint scent of damp stone.

She found Devak near the entrance, a gaunt man with a weary expression that made him look far older than his years. He was adjusting the oil lamps used as backup for the main beacon, his movements precise and methodical.

"Are you here to sightsee or to satisfy your curiosity about ghosts?" he asked without looking up.

Ananya smiled. "A bit of both. I'm a marine biologist, but I've heard some...interesting stories about this place."

Devak's eyes met hers, and for a moment, she saw something she couldn't quite place—fear, perhaps, or resignation. "The sea holds many secrets, and so does this lighthouse," he said. "But some truths are better left buried."

She tried to probe further, but he dismissed her questions, retreating into the tower. As she turned to leave, she noticed something strange—a faint, melodic humming carried by the wind. It seemed to come from the lighthouse itself, but when she paused to listen, it faded away.

Chapter 4: The First Sign

That night, Ananya dreamed of the lighthouse. In her dream, its light swept across the dark waves, revealing ghostly figures rising from the depths. A shadowy form stood at the top of the tower, beckoning her.

She woke with a start, her heart racing. The sound of the humming from earlier lingered in her mind, as if it had followed her into her dreams. Unable to shake the unease, she decided to return to the lighthouse the next day.

This time, Devak was not outside. She ventured into the tower, her footsteps echoing on the spiral staircase. The air grew colder as she climbed, and the faint scent of seawater grew stronger. At the top, she found the beacon room.

The large glass panes offered a panoramic view of the ocean, but what caught her attention was a notebook lying on the console. Its pages were filled with hastily scrawled notes—warnings, pleas, and descriptions of the same humming she had heard.

Before she could read further, a low moan filled the air. It wasn't the wind; it was too human, too mournful. She spun around, but the room was empty. Suddenly, the beacon flickered, casting eerie shadows across the walls.

She fled, clutching the notebook, her mind racing with questions.

Chapter 5: The Keeper's Tale

Back in her cottage, Ananya examined the notebook. The entries were fragmented and disjointed, but one name appeared repeatedly: "Amara."

"Amara calls to me. Her voice rises with the tide."
"I see her at the edge of the rocks. She is waiting."
"Forgive me, Amara."

The entries became increasingly erratic, with lines scratched out and smudged. At the bottom of one page, in large, bold letters, it read: *"DO NOT ANSWER THE LIGHT."*

The cryptic notes gnawed at her curiosity. The next morning, she confronted Devak at the village pier, where he was collecting supplies. He froze when he saw the notebook in her hands.

"Where did you get that?" he demanded, his voice low but trembling with anger.

"I found it in the beacon room," she replied. "Who is Amara? And what's happening in that lighthouse?"

Devak looked around as if fearing they were being watched. Finally, he gestured for her to follow him to a secluded spot near the dunes.

"Amara was my wife," he began, his voice heavy with grief. "She drowned near the lighthouse five years ago during a storm. I was the keeper then. I failed to save her."

He paused, his eyes glistening. "After her death, strange things started happening. The light flickered even when there was no power outage. At night, I heard her voice calling my name. Others who took the job after me said the same. Some of them couldn't take it—they left. Others...didn't make it out alive."

"Why stay, then?" Ananya asked.

"Because I owe her," he said simply. "I couldn't save her then. Maybe this is my chance to set things right."

His words sent a chill down Ananya's spine, but they also strengthened her resolve. If the haunting had roots in Amara's death, then perhaps understanding her story could bring peace to the lighthouse—and to Devak.

Chapter 6: The Sea's Secret

That evening, Ananya decided to explore the cliffs below the lighthouse. The tide was low, revealing jagged rocks and small pools where marine life thrived. She noticed a narrow path winding down the cliffside, barely visible through the overgrowth.

As she descended, the air grew colder, and a sense of unease settled over her. The waves crashed against the rocks with deafening force, but beneath the roar, she thought she heard something else—a faint, melodic humming.

At the base of the cliff, she found a small cave partially hidden by the tide. Inside, the walls were covered with strange, swirling patterns carved into the stone. In the center of the cave lay a pile of debris—rotting wood, rusted nails, and fragments of a shattered lantern.

Among the wreckage, she found a locket. Inside was a faded photograph of a woman with kind eyes and a gentle smile. Ananya's breath caught in her throat. This must be Amara.

The humming grew louder, reverberating through the cave. Ananya turned toward the entrance and froze. A shadowy figure stood silhouetted against the fading light, its form flickering like a reflection on water.

Before she could react, the figure dissolved, leaving only the echo of its presence. Clutching the locket, Ananya scrambled back up the cliff, her heart pounding.

Chapter 7: The Light Beckons

That night, Ananya returned to the lighthouse with the locket. Devak was waiting for her, his expression a mixture of dread and hope.

"I found this," she said, handing him the locket.

Devak's hands trembled as he opened it. "This was hers," he whispered. Tears streamed down his face as he stared at the photograph.

Ananya told him about the cave and the figure she had seen. "I think Amara's spirit is tied to the lighthouse—and to you," she said gently. "She's trying to reach you."

Devak nodded slowly. "I've felt it. Every time the light turns toward the sea, I hear her voice. But I'm afraid. What if answering her only brings more pain?"

Ananya placed a hand on his shoulder. "Maybe it's time to face her. Together."

That night, under a moonlit sky, they climbed to the beacon room. Devak lit the lantern, and they watched as its beam swept across the dark waves.

The humming returned, louder and more melodic than ever. Slowly, the light began to flicker, casting eerie shadows on the walls. Devak stepped forward, his voice breaking as he called out, "Amara! I'm here!"

The air grew heavy, and the shadows coalesced into a shimmering figure. It was Amara, her form translucent but unmistakable. Her eyes locked onto Devak, filled with both sorrow and love.

"You left me," she said, her voice a haunting whisper.

"I'm sorry," Devak choked. "I tried to save you, but I failed. Please forgive me."

Amara reached out, her hand hovering inches from his. "You must let me go," she said softly. "The sea has claimed me, but it's not your burden to carry anymore."

Chapter 8: Farewell

As the first light of dawn broke over the horizon, Amara's figure began to fade. The humming softened, replaced by the gentle lapping of the waves against the rocks.

Devak stood motionless, tears streaming down his face. Ananya placed a reassuring hand on his arm. "She's at peace now," she said.

He nodded, his shoulders sagging with relief and exhaustion. "And so am I," he murmured.

In the days that followed, Devak resigned from his post as lighthouse keeper, passing the responsibility to someone new. The lighthouse, once shrouded in darkness and mystery, now stood as a beacon of hope—a reminder of love, loss, and redemption.

Chapter 9: The Final Note

Ananya wrote a feature article about the lighthouse, blending its haunting tale with her own experiences. The story garnered widespread attention, drawing visitors to Velas who wished to see the infamous Kaala Rekha Lighthouse for themselves.

Despite its newfound fame, the lighthouse remained a solemn place. Ananya often visited the cliffs, finding solace in the sound of the waves and the memory of Amara's voice.

Chapter 10: Echoes of the Sea

On her last day in Velas, Ananya climbed the lighthouse one final time. The beacon room was quiet, bathed in the warm glow of the setting sun.

As she stood by the window, she heard a faint humming, carried on the wind like a distant melody. A smile touched her lips. "Goodbye, Amara," she whispered.

The light turned toward the sea, and for a brief moment, Ananya thought she saw a figure standing on the waves, its form shimmering like the horizon. Then it was gone, leaving only the echoes of the sea and the promise of new beginnings.

Dear Readers,

Thank you for joining me on this journey through the eerie tales of this book. Each story in this collection was written with the hope of igniting your imagination, stirring your emotions, and perhaps leaving you with a lingering sense of wonder—or unease.

Stories have a unique way of connecting us, and I hope these tales brought you moments of reflection and excitement, as they did for me while writing them. If these pages inspired even a single chill down your spine or made you pause to glance over your shoulder, then my purpose as a storyteller is fulfilled.

I would love to hear your thoughts, interpretations, or even your own experiences with the supernatural. Feel free to reach out or share your feedback—I believe every story grows richer when shared.

Until we meet again in the world of words, remember: shadows may fall, but light always finds a way.

Warm regards,
Ravinderr Singh.

Connect at- akkyxyz007@gmail.com